To those who have faced scarier foes
than dragons in the fight for love
— DH

For my mother, whose selfless love inspires
me to be open, kind and loving to others
— SL

A STUDIO PRESS BOOK
First published in the UK in 2020 by Studio Press,
an imprint of Bonnier Books UK,
The Plaza, 535 King's Road, London SW10 0SZ
www.studiopressbooks.co.uk   www.bonnierbooks.co.uk

© 2020 Studio Press Books

Text copyright © 2018 by Daniel Haack Illustrations copyright © 2018 by Stevie Lewis

Printed and bound in China

First Edition 10 9 8 7 6 5 4 3 2 1
A CIP catalogue for this book is available from the British Library

ISBN 978-17874-1-825-7

Published in partnership with GLAAD.
A portion of the proceeds from the
sale of this book will be donated
to accelerating LGBTQ acceptance.
glaad.org

FSC
www.fsc.org
MIX
Paper from
responsible sources
FSC® C144853

Prince & Knight

words by Daniel Haack
pictures by Stevie Lewis

STUDIO PRESS

Once upon a time,
in a kingdom far from here,

lived a charming prince
who was handsome and sincere.

His parents knew that soon, it would be time he took the throne.
But with a kingdom so grand, the prince could not rule alone.

So the three of them set out and travelled far and wide,
on a quest to find the prince a kind and worthy bride.

The prince met many ladies
(and made the maidens swoon!),

but soon it was clear
he was singing a different tune.

"Thank you," he told his parents. "I appreciate you tried,
but I'm looking for something different in a partner by my side."

But while the royals were away,
their land faced quite a scare
from a dragon fast approaching,
breathing fire everywhere!

All the villagers ran in fear!
Even the soldiers hid and fled.
"This vicious beast is far too great.
We must retreat or we'll be dead!"

The prince heard the dreadful news,
and he raced home with all his might.
To protect his precious realm,
the prince was ready for a fight.

Alas! Before you fear our prince
had to face the beast alone . . .

along on horseback
came a knight.
To the prince he was
unknown.

The dragon charged upon our heroes,
thinking it had already won,
but the knight had a bold idea,
and raised his shield to face the sun.

The glare hit the shining metal, blinding the dragon's fiery eyes,
but it was what the prince did next that really caught it by surprise!

The prince had climbed atop the dragon
and tied a rope around its head.

He wrapped the cord around the neck
and down the body like a thread.

The plan had worked! The dragon was caught.
Its body was tied and bound,
but the prince up high had lost his grip
and was falling to the ground!

The knight below jumped on his horse
and they began to race.

The prince was caught and free from harm,
held in the knight's embrace.

"You saved my life!"
"And you saved mine!"
They said to one another.

And in a flash, to each it felt
there simply was no other.

The knight took off his helmet
to reveal his handsome face,

and as they gazed
into each other's eyes,
their hearts
began to race.

As the villagers returned,
it became clear to those around
that the prince's one true love
had at last been surely found.

The king and queen
had come back too,
and were overwhelmed
with joy.

"We have finally
found someone
who is perfect
for our boy!"

And on the two men's wedding day,
the air filled with cheer and laughter,
for the prince and his shining knight
would live happily ever after.

DANIEL HAACK began writing at a young age, although much of his earliest work centred exclusively around his desire to be a swashbuckling hero. Like the Prince and the Knight, he just wants to save the day and get the boy, too. He has since written for various publications and collections, and *Prince & Knight* is his debut children's book. He graduated from Ithaca College and now works in children's educational media, for which he won a Daytime Emmy Award. Originally from Mount Horeb, Wisconsin, and formerly a New Yorker, Daniel now lives in Los Angeles, California, USA.

danielhaack.com

STEVIE LEWIS has been living on the road for the past two years, furthering her passion for climbing, art and the outdoors. Striving to live simply and tread lightly on the earth, she gathers inspiration from a variety of adventures, be it climbing in the high desert in central Oregon, hiking through the wilderness of Alaska, or sharing laughs with fellow travellers around a campfire. After working for years in animation, she now illustrates children's books and creates art based on her travels.

chocosweete.com